D0561096

FINN REEDER FLU FIGHTER

by Eric Stevens   illustrated by Kay Fraser

How I Survived a Worldwide Pandemic, the School Bully, and the Craziest Game of Dodge Ball Ever

Finn Reeder
Eighth Grade
Age 13
5'5", 110 pounds
Strengths: Really good at checkers, amazing at video games, nice to animals
Weaknesses: Dodge ball, talking to girls, avoiding Vic Dooker (school bully)

STONE ARCH BOOKS
a capstone imprint

Published by Stone Arch Books
A Capstone Imprint
151 Good Counsel Drive, P.O. Box 669
Mankato, Minnesota 56002
www.capstonepub.com

Printed in the United States of America in Stevens Point, Wisconsin.
112009
005641R

Library of Congress Cataloging-in-Publication Data is available
on the Library of Congress website.

Trade hardcover ISBN: 978-1-4342-2562-7

Creative Director: Heather Kindseth
Art Director/Graphic Designer: Kay Fraser
Photo Credits: Shutterstock/Ferenc Szelepcsenyi

MY JOURNAL

Ms. Westing's

window

closet

Pink Fred Vic Finn (me)

X

Graham Dewey Louis Amy

exit door

3rd Period
Journal Project
March 1 - March 30

4

English Class

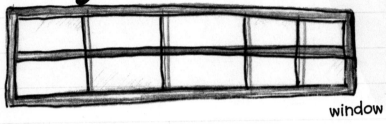

window

Gus   Jessie   Jake   Zoe

Henry   Jenni   Lexi   Helena

teacher's desk

bookshelves

WEEK

1

SO FAR:
Stupid assignments: 1

MONDAY March 1

This is stupid.

I'm sorry, Ms. Westing. I don't know if this was your assignment or if the sub made it up himself. He says you left it for us, in your notes. He says you'd been planning for this assignment since the beginning of the year.

I say he's a liar. I say the Ms. Westing I know wouldn't make us keep a journal with a full page for every single day.

Mr. Grumble — that's the sub — was obviously making it up as he went along. I even asked him if I could illustrate the entries. You know, for clarity. He didn't have an answer ready! If you had written out this assignment for us, you would have included all the necessary information. Right?

Did I mention he had a booger hanging from his left nostril all day? Because he did.

But fine. So here's what happened today:

Ms. Westing wasn't in English class and we have to write a journal now. Every day.

Vic Dooker laughed when Mr. Grumble said you were out, Ms. W. He said his aunt works in the attendance office. She told him you have that new flu everyone has been talking about. Bird or pig or elephant or some kind of animal.

Well, I had the flu last winter. I was back in school after only three days. So I'm sure you'll be up on your feet soon. Then you can kick Mr. Grumble out of here. And we can stop keeping these journals!

Oh, also I noticed Jenni Richter isn't in class either. I wonder if she has elephant flu too. . . .

Yours truly,

FINN REEDER

TUESDAY
March 2

Mr. Grumble was our English sub again, so I guess you're still sick, Ms. Westing. Drink plenty of fluids.

Today Mr. Grumble partnered me with Vic Dooker for a poetry project. We had to read a poem to each other and then discuss it. But every time I started reading, Vic would make fart sounds with his armpit.

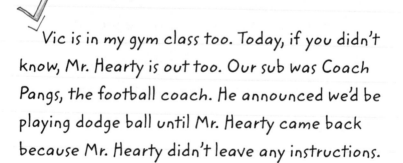

Vic is in my gym class too. Today, if you didn't know, Mr. Hearty is out too. Our sub was Coach Pangs, the football coach. He announced we'd be playing dodge ball until Mr. Hearty came back because Mr. Hearty didn't leave any instructions.

I'm telling you, Ms. Westing. Vic looked right at me and sneered. He has it in for me.

Vic's usual expression

Also, Jenni Richter still isn't back in school. Today Henry Gluck was out too. And two kids weren't in gym class.

You know, if it means I'd miss dodge ball, I think I feel a little feverish myself. . . .

Yours truly,

FINN REEDER

WEDNESDAY
March 3

Mr. Grumble is probably the worst sub of all time. First of all, he wouldn't let us put our desks in a circle even though it's Wednesday. We tried to tell him Wednesday is discussion day, but he wouldn't listen. (You should probably be clearer in your notes from now on, Ms. Westing!)

Then he made everyone move up to the front of the room. I should probably explain that there were five empty desks in the front row. That's because in addition to Jenni and Henry, there were four new absent kids today: Louis, Dewey, Pink, and Graham.

According to Vic, all of them have that swine flu he said you have. Mr. Grumble said we should call it H1N1, not swine flu. Then of course Vic started yelling, "Oink, oink!"

Anyway, right after we all moved up and settled in, Mr. Grumble opened his mouth to speak, and instead he sneezed all over everyone! I don't think I got the worst of the spray. Ick.

Vic came after me in gym class, just like I knew he would. Before Coach Pangs could even blow the starting whistle, a red ball slammed into my belly. I thought I was going to die, for real. But I just fell on the floor and lay there for a while. Eventually Vic stopped laughing and started throwing at some other kids.

The big news came during last period. Principal Toomey announced over the PA that we're officially in the middle of a flu pandemic. The President called a national emergency!

I'm sure my parents won't overreact.

Hopefully,

FINN REEDER

My parents have overreacted. Last night when I got home, my dad was standing in the doorway wearing a surgeon's mask. I'm not kidding. And he only opened the door long enough for me to come inside. Then he sprayed me and the doorknob and the door with disinfectant spray.

Now I'm being forced to wear one of those masks to school. I'm embarrassed, but the good news is I'm not the only one. Amy Fleur is wearing one too.

Which brings me to the good news. Mr. Grumble wasn't our sub today. Instead, Ms. Pipslink was. I guess Mr. Grumble has the flu too!

That's what Vic said, at least.

So, like I was saying, Ms. Pipslink is a lot nicer than Mr. Grumble. We had to partner up again for reading. Ms. Pipslink didn't make Vic my partner. What more can I ask for?

Today I was partnered with Amy, which is when I realized I wasn't the only person wearing a dumb mask. I mean, I would rather have been partnered with Jake Dinny or Gus Tattle, but they were both out today. I saw Jake's little brother Skippy on the bus this morning. Jake has swine flu too. I mean, H1N1.

So Amy and I had to read this short story about the end of the world. It was pretty cool, but we didn't get the ending at all.

Confused,

FINN REEDER

Friday! Ms. Pipslink is our sub again today. Since it's Friday, she said we could sit in a circle. No one bothered to tell her that we usually sit in a circle on Wednesday.

There were only ten of us in class. It doesn't really seem like it matters anymore where we sit.

I decided to keep track of how many people are out sick and who's still healthy. You can see for yourself. Don't feel bad, by the way. All my classes are mostly empty. I heard that more than half the teachers are out sick, too.

In other news, Vic attacked me in gym class again. Coach Pangs seems very healthy. No flu symptoms there. I've never seen a grown man laugh so hard at a kid (me) getting hit in the butt by a ball (thrown by Vic).

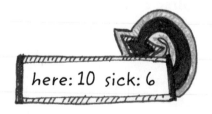

here: 10 sick: 6

I wish Coach Pangs would get this flu. Maybe our next gym sub will want to play checkers or something.

At least it's Friday. My friend Greg and I are supposed to go to the mall. The new video game *DragonFlight III* is out. So is that new horror movie, *Mummy at Midnight.* Maybe I'll write a review of the game and the movie in the journal. It'll take up some space!

Excited about the weekend,

FINN REEDER

SATURDAY
March 6

This is so far the worst Saturday of all time. Luckily I'm going to bed after I write this, so I guess nothing else bad could happen.

First of all, Dad has completely lost his mind. Now we all have to wear the masks all the time, even in the house. He's also walking around with that disinfectant spray twenty-four hours a day! If he sees me scratch my ear or wipe my nose with my hand, he jumps up and sprays me all over.

This morning Dad took me to the medical supply store. He bought three of those bright orange hazardous-materials suits like the ones they wear on TV when they examine aliens. Dad put his on in the parking lot! Then we went to the grocery store. I refused to put my suit on, so Dad made me wait in the car. That was fine with me. I didn't want to be seen with my crazy dad in his hazmat suit!

Anyway, he stocked up like there was a zombie invasion going on. He bought cans and cans of soup and vegetables and chili and stew . . . and that was just the beginning.

There was bottled water, first-aid supplies, and bottles of cold and cough medicine. He bought a humidifier, a dehumidifier, bandages, a tank of propane, a bundle of firewood, five bags of ice, and ten jumbo bottles of water.

"Dad!" I said after he'd loaded up the trunk and the backseat. "It's just the flu, not the end of the world!"

Dad climbed into the driver's seat. Then he pulled off his hazmat hood and faced me. "Son, this is a worldwide epidemic," he said. "This is very serious. If we're not prepared, we're done for."

"Prepared for what?" I asked.

As we drove toward the exit, he shrugged. "Anything," he said. "Looters, vandals, destruction. We could be looking at years underground."

I want to go back to school.

Sadly,

FINN REEDER

I was wrong. Something bad did happen after I went to bed last night.

I was all cozy and fast asleep. Then Dad started shouting. "Looters! Vandals! Zombies! Flu victims are attacking! To the safe room!"

I jumped out of bed and tripped on my covers. I ended up tangled in my sheets on my bedroom floor.

Dad came barging in, ringing a bell, still shouting. "Wake up, Finn! Get up off the floor! To the safe room!" he screamed.

I didn't even know we had a safe room. Dad scrambled out of my room. I managed to get up and run downstairs in time to see Dad and Mom heading into the basement.

All the food and water he'd bought was lined up on the shelves. A small propane stove was set up in the corner. Dad closed the door at the bottom of the steps and locked it with a padlock. Then he looked at his watch.

"That wasn't bad," he said. "But we have to be quicker. If crazed flu victims are breaking down the door to steal our propane or our ice, we won't have a moment to spare!"

"This was a drill?" I shouted. "I was sleeping!"

Dad smiled and nodded. "They're bound to strike at night, Finn," he said. Then he unlocked the door and I ran up to bed.

And now it's Sunday night. Like I said, I wanted to go with Greg to the mall. You could be reading a review of *Mummy at Midnight* right now instead of the story of my dad's insanity. But when I told Mom I was going to meet Greg at the mall, she said no way. There was too big a risk of infection in such a crowded place.

I don't know. I guess Dad must have gotten to her.

Very annoyed,

FINN REEDER

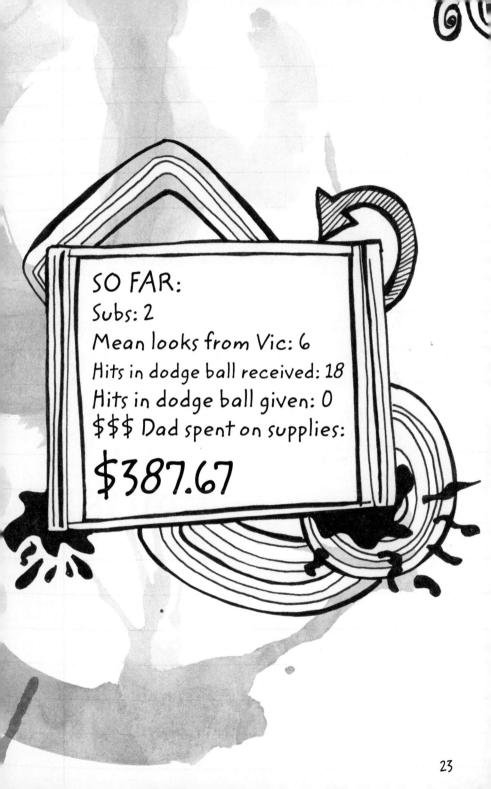

SO FAR:
Subs: 2
Mean looks from Vic: 6
Hits in dodge ball received: 18
Hits in dodge ball given: 0
$$$ Dad spent on supplies:

$387.67

Me looking lame with my mask on

Whew. Back at school.

It's nice to be out of the crazy house. Dad ran another drill this morning at four a.m.! It was still dark out!

Anyway, school is definitely quieter. In fact, it's a little freaky. There are only eight of us in your class today, Ms. Westing. Ms. Pipslink is still our sub, too.

We all clapped when she came in. When she asked why we were clapping, Vic said, "We're impressed you survived the weekend in this epidemic."

FLU EPIDEMIC REACHES CIT

March 7 - Officials said today that the sweeping the nation is at epidemic lev Across the city, hundreds of citizens become ill. Mayor Randolph apolog for the fact that no vaccines are yet avail saying that the city was delivered a ship of bird-flu vaccine instead of swin vaccine. "It was a mistake anyone make," the mayor said.

here: 8 sick: 8

All my teachers are out sick now. We have a sub in every single class. And most classes are almost empty of students, too. Amy says if this keeps up, they might as well close the school. There's no point in paying all these subs if there are so few students.

In gym, Coach Pangs, still in perfect health, announced he was sick of dodge ball. At first Vic was disappointed, until Coach Pangs announced our new activity: wrestling. Of course, he partnered me with Vic.

Boing

I don't want to talk about it,

FINN REEDER

TUESDAY
March 9

I guess Ms. Pipslink finally gave in and got sick too. We had a new sub today for your class: Kirk.

Yup, Kirk. He asked us to call him by his first name. Also, he was wearing jeans and a baseball cap. I guess they'll hire anyone to sub nowadays, because he sure didn't seem like a teacher to me.

First of all, he sat on the floor! He asked us to also sit on the floor, if we wanted to, but none of us did. Then he recited Shakespeare to us, from memory! It was the weirdest thing I've ever seen happen at school.

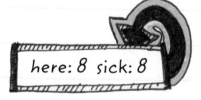

here: 8 sick: 8

And that's all that happened. The whole hour. Kirk, on the floor, in his baseball cap, playing both parts in Romeo and Juliet.

Kirk
~~JULIET~~: O think'st thou we shall ever meet again?

Kirk
~~ROMEO~~: I doubt it not; and all these woes shall serve
For sweet discourses in our time to come.

Kirk
~~JULIET~~: O God, I have an ill-divining soul!
Methinks I see thee, now thou art below,
As one dead in the bottom of a tomb:
Either my eyesight fails, or thou look'st pale.

Kirk
~~ROMEO~~: And trust me, love, in my eye so do you:
Dry sorrow drinks our blood. Adieu, adieu!

What light through yonder window barfs,

FINN REEDER

March 10

Greg has the locker next to mine, so I see him most mornings. Today he didn't show up. I saw Katie Bobbit coming down the main hall. She rides his bus.

"Hey, Katie," I called to her. "Wasn't Greg on the bus today?"

She shook her head, but she didn't come very close to me. When she spoke, she covered her mouth with her hand. Of course, I was wearing that dumb mask, so I didn't worry about germs.

"Nope," she said through her hand. "My mom said that his mom said he had a bad fever last night, and he's definitely got the H1N1."

"Oh no," I said. "Not Greg too!"

here: 7 sick: 9

"Hey, you're his best friend, aren't you?" Katie asked.

I nodded. She backed away even farther. "Um, stay away from me," she said. A look of panic fell over her face.

I laughed. "No, Katie," I said. "I'm not sick."

She jumped back, and started pointing at me. "Get him away from me! Help! Help!" She threw down her books and ran away.

"Katie!" I called after her. Then I realized everyone in the hallway was staring at me. I tried to laugh it off, saying, "She's crazy, huh?"

They kept staring.

"Really, I'm not sick," I said. "I haven't seen Greg in ages. For real."

No one replied. No one even moved. So I just grabbed my stuff and headed to my first class.

Really, definitely not sick,

FINN REEDER

This is officially nuts.

No one is acting like themselves. People won't go anywhere near me in the halls. Well, they won't go anywhere near each other, either. But I think they're being extra weird to me, thanks to what Katie said in the hall yesterday.

Did I mention Katie is home sick today? I don't know if she actually has the flu. I think some kids aren't coming because they're afraid to get the flu. The point is, I think a lot of kids saw her freak out about me. Now she's out sick. They're making their own connections, I guess, and blaming me.

It's time to put a stop to this. First of all, Kirk is out of control. Today he rapped for us. He set up a "boom box," put on some very cheesy beats, and rapped at us. About Shakespeare.

here: 6 sick: 10

Also, there are now only six of us in class, and English is the most crowded of my classes right now. You should see my history class. It's just me, Arnie Finkle, and Kim Giblet. The sub today was Nelson. I bet you know him. He's the guy who usually guards the parking lot. He wore his security uniform and everything.

Anyway, I don't have a plan yet, but I'll come up with one. This flu insanity must be stopped!

With determination,

So, today was . . . interesting. I think I have to give up on keeping track of your class, Ms. Westing. See, Principal Toomey announced that since so few kids were in school, and since so few teachers were in school, we'd be combining classes.

What this means is that Kirk has been sent home. Or maybe he got the flu.

So today, class was kind of full. It was a nice change. There were almost twenty of us, including me, Vic, Amy, and Fred Wendt from your class.

Our sub was Dr. Gray. Yup, we went from a sub in jeans who wanted us to call him Kirk to a doctor! She seems nice at least. And I'm happy to say she was wearing a mask, too.

"See that?" I said. "Dr. Gray is wearing a mask. And she's a doctor!"

Everyone looked at me, and then at the teacher in her mask, and then at Amy in her mask.

here: 4 sick: 12

Dr. Gray laughed. "I'm not that kind of doctor," she said. "My degree is in literature. But you're right. It's a good idea to wear a mask during a pandemic."

After English, Amy caught up to me in the hallway. "Walk with me to the gym?" she said. "I don't want to walk with anyone who isn't wearing a mask."

I shrugged. "Okay," I said. "Don't you feel silly with that thing on? My dad is making me wear it. He's really lost it," I added, shaking my head.

"I don't mind," Amy said. "After all, you and I have been wearing these things for a while, and we're not sick yet, right?"

Just then Vic ran by and knocked my books and Amy's books to the floor. "Bully!" Amy shouted as Vic ran on, laughing.

"At least you don't have to wrestle him," I said.

From behind my mask,

FINN REEDER

SATURDAY

March 13

I am sick of this house, Ms. Westing.

Dad won't even let me open the windows now, never mind actually step out onto the front lawn.

This morning at around 11, Dad went to the front door and peeked out the little window next to it. He just stood there, staring, for like forty-five minutes. Finally, he shushed Mom and me and uncapped his disinfectant spray.

Then the mail slot swung open. Some envelopes fell to the floor. Even before the slot fell closed again, Dad was spraying disinfectant all over it.

"That postal service worker wasn't following pandemic rules," Dad said. "He should be wearing gloves until the virus is under control."

With the mail in his gloved hand, Dad headed for the kitchen. A big roasting tray was ready on the stove. "Don't get too close without a mask on," Dad said.

cans of spray used by Dad: 9

He pulled on his hazmat hood. Mom and I stood in the doorway of the kitchen, watching.

Dad dropped the mail into the roasting tray. Then he grabbed the box of kitchen matches Mom uses to light birthday candles. He pulled out one long match, lit it, and dropped it into the roasting tray.

The mail immediately burst into flames.

"Are you crazy?" I said. "There might have been something important in there!"

"Crazy like a fox," he replied, smiling as he watched the mail burn to ashes. "Nothing could be more important than our health, Finn. You know that."

Mom and I shook our heads and backed out slowly.

Seriously, I am so sick of being in this house.

Going stir crazy,

FINN REEDER

SUNDAY
March 14

Great news, Ms. Westing! I'm not sick of being in my house anymore. I'm only sick of my room. I've been stuck in here for the last twenty-four hours!

That's right. I'm under arrest in my own room, Dad's orders. I'm only allowed out to use the bathroom. Then he follows me the whole way, spraying a cloud of disinfectant around me as I go.

As long as I refuse to wear one of those hazmat suits, he says he'll keep spraying.

Dad delivers meals to my room. He opens the door for a split second and I watch his gloved hand drop a bowl of macaroni and cheese or a plate of waffles on the rug. Then the door closes again and Dad calls out, "Bon appetit!"

You're probably wondering why my dad would be acting like this. Or maybe you're assuming I got the flu and he's protecting himself.

Nope. Mom got the flu! She's in bed, and I'm being kept locked away for my own good. Only Dad, protected by his crazy suit, is allowed to roam freely.

I managed to get a peek at Mom during one of my scheduled trips to pee. Dad set up one of those plastic bubble tents in their room! She's completely cut off from the air in the house. When it's time for her to eat, Dad goes in and unzips the bubble. Then he uses a mechanical arm to put the food in front of her. I don't even know where he got the mechanical arm! Mom has to hold her breath until the bubble is zipped back up.

I think once this flu scare is over, we'll have to take Dad to the doctor. Not because he might have the flu — because he might be totally nuts!

Son of a crazy man,

FINN REEDER

WEEK

3

SO FAR:
Subs in English: 4
Wrestling matches: 15
Wrestling matches won: 0
Times my nose was in Vic's armpit: 4

Amy: cute

MONDAY ?

March 15

This must have been a bad weekend for everyone, I guess. Today, even the combined English class is tiny. Plus, we have yet another sub. Unfortunately, I didn't get his name. I'm not sure he even told us his name. See, he was wearing a mask, and not one of those paper masks like Amy and I wear. He was wearing a full gas mask.

Now that I think about it, I'm not even sure our sub was a man!

He (or she or it) said some things in the beginning of class, but we didn't understand any of it. It came out sounding like something between radio static and the old air conditioner in our living room.

Eventually, all the students just took out our books and started reading. Then the sub sat down. Maybe it went to sleep. I couldn't see its eyes.

Gas Mask Sub: day 1

I spent most of the class doodling cartoons for Amy. Then she would add captions to them. For example, I drew a picture of Principal Toomey, and Amy added a talk bubble.

At least there are some fun things at school,

FINN REEDER

TUESDAY
March 16

Let me set this up for you, Ms. Westing, because you won't believe it. I saw it, and I don't even believe it.

Amy and I were walking to the cafeteria after our fourth period math class. Our math sub let us out a few minutes early after Vic sneezed. I'm pretty sure Vic was faking, but it sure scared that sub.

As Amy and I passed the front of the school, two cars pulled up. Principal Toomey came rushing past us. He was holding a handkerchief over his mouth and only glanced at Amy and me for an instant. Then he pushed through the doors.

"I told your boss to send you to the side doors!" he shouted. But I guess the drivers didn't hear him. They both got out of their cars and started unloading something from the backseats.

When Amy and I realized what it was, we were shocked.

Gas Mask Sub: day 2

Delivery Receipt
Antonello's Pizzeria
We Like Pizza!
March 16

15 large pies...$10.00 each

Total: $150.00

Deliver to East Middle
Principal Toomey

I hope you're sitting down. The drivers unloaded fifteen large pizzas! Right there in front of the school.

Principal Toomey gave them lots of money for the pizzas. Then he asked me and Amy to help him carry the pies to the cafeteria.

"And don't make a scene!" he snapped at us. "If the other students see these pizzas before we reach the lunch line, there will be chaos! Rioting!"

He reminded me of my dad.

Of course, Amy and I were the first students to get our pizza. I had three slices.

Oh, by the way, the entire cafeteria staff is out with the flu.

Two slices of pepperoni and one veggie,

FINN REEDER

In English, we had Gas Mask Sub again. We got into class and all of the desks were in a circle. Then Gas Mask Sub talked for a while. We didn't understand a word of it.

But then I caught Vic staring at me. And not in a nice way, either. Just before the bell rang, he even sneered.

When we got to gym, I figured out why. Coach Pangs had a new activity planned for us: fencing.

Pirates! Robin Hood! Swordplay! It sounds fun! But with Vic? Do you think Vic was interested in learning how to fence? No. Vic was interested in hitting me repeatedly with a sword.

At one point, Vic had me up against the bleachers. I swear, he would have stabbed me right through the heart. Then suddenly, Amy came from out of nowhere.

"Quit it, you bully!" she shouted. Then she punched Vic right in the arm.

Gas Mask Sub: day 3

Vic started screaming. Then he rolled up his sleeve. There was a huge bruise!

I looked at Amy. "Wow," I said. "You're a superhero!"

Vic rolled his eyes. "She didn't give me this bruise," he said. "This is from my vaccine shot!"

Now we were really shocked. No vaccines had gotten through to our town and everyone knew it.

"How did you get a vaccine?!" Amy asked.

"Last weekend I went out to my aunt's place in Creekville," Vic said. "They had tons of shots."

"Well, that explains why you're not sick even though you didn't wear a mask," I said.

"More importantly," Amy said, "we know your weakness. So you better stop picking on Finn in gym class!"

My hero.

Happily,

FINN REEDER

Gas Mask is our sub again. Today he or she or it was in a full orange hazmat suit. I'm beginning to wonder if Gas Mask is actually my father.

Amy brought in a newspaper article about H1N1. It said vaccines are finally coming to our local clinic. They should be here in the next week. By then it will be almost four weeks late, of course. I guess better late than never.

The article also said that most people who get H1N1 are over the flu in a few days. This flu rarely causes any real problems. In fact, the article said the normal old seasonal flu that some people get in the winter is actually more dangerous. I mean, according to the statistics.

I was pointing that out to Amy. Then she looked me in the eye and I noticed her eyes were a little red, kind of like she hadn't slept well.

"Are you okay?" I asked. "You look tired."

Gas Mask Sub: day 4

Her eyes opened really wide for a second. Then she went back to reading the article.

"Amy, I think we should spread this news around," I said. "Let's make copies of this article and send them home with kids. People are really overreacting to this flu!"

Amy glanced at me quickly. Then she picked up the article and shoved it into my hands. "Go ahead," she said.

Then the weirdest thing happened. She got up from her desk, lifted off her mask, pulled a tissue from her pocket, and sneezed.

Gas Mask looked up suddenly. Fred, Vic, and I all stared at Amy.

She looked right at me. "I'm sorry," she said. Then she ran from the room.

I guess the masks aren't the perfect solution we thought they were.

Still wearing a mask just in case,

FINN REEDER

FRIDAY

March 19

Gas Mask was here again today.

Only Vic, Fred, and I were in class. Gas Mask didn't bother trying to lecture or teach anything. Vic and Fred and I sat as far apart from each other as possible. No one spoke. We just sat there. We glared at each other now and then.

I sat with my arms folded. Amy was home sick. If Vic tried anything, I'd have to find that sweet spot on his right arm myself.

I glanced at Vic. He glared back.

Vic looked at Gas Mask. Gas Mask didn't move.

Gas Mask Sub: day 5

Fred looked at me. I looked at Fred.

Vic glared at Fred. Fred looked everywhere but at Vic.

Fred sniffled.

Fred took a deep breath.

Gas Mask, Vic, and I looked at Fred.

Fred sneezed.

All alone with Vic,

FINN REEDER

March 20

I'm back under arrest in my room. Mom is still sick, I assume. I haven't really seen her since last Saturday. We did wave at each other briefly this morning, but then Dad slammed the door and kept us apart.

You probably know all about this, Ms. Westing. It's been all over the news, and I assume you're watching TV. If I was at home sick for almost three weeks, I'd watch plenty of TV.

Luckily, Dad let me bring a TV into my room when I threatened to run away. Anyway, according to the news the epidemic has reached its peak. That means things should start getting better now.

So with that news, and with the vaccines on the way, hopefully soon everything will be back to normal.

I got an email from Amy. She said her whole family has H1N1 now. Her fever is 102 degrees, she's sneezing all the time, and she can hardly breathe. She also said, "I hope I didn't get you sick. Punch Vic in the arm for me."

At least the computer still works,

FINN REEDER

March 21

Well, it looks like my room arrest is over. That's because I'm now the only one well enough to take care of the house and cook meals.

Dad got the flu.

I can hardly believe it! I mean, no one was more careful than Dad. He even wore that dumb hazmat suit to bed.

It must have happened one time when Mom was getting a meal and the bubble was unzipped. Maybe she sneezed at the wrong moment, or maybe Dad forgot to wear gloves when he picked up her dishes or something.

Anyway, today was super tiring. I got up thinking I'd spend another lazy day trapped in my room. Instead, I woke up to my phone ringing.

"Hello?" I said. I looked at the clock. It wasn't even six a.m.

"Finn, this is your father," Dad said.

"Where are you?" I asked.

"I'm in bed, in the next room," Dad answered. "I called you from my cell phone."

"Why?" I asked.

"I'm afraid the flu has finally gotten to me," Dad said sadly. "You're the man of the house now."

"Are you kidding?" I said.

"I don't kid," Dad said. "Not about worldwide epidemics."

He went on to tell me how I'd have to make all the meals, feed him and Mom, and do all the spraying with disinfectant. He insisted I put on the second hazmat suit.

Monday can't come soon enough.

The man of the house,

FINN REEDER

SO FAR:
Days of Gas Mask Sub: 5
People left in class: 2
(no more Fred)
People sick in my family: 2

Amy: sick :(

MONDAY

March 22

Everyone is gone.

Gas Mask is here, of course, wearing the orange hazmat suit, and so are exactly two students.

Me.

And Vic.

He's watching me. I know he is. I bet his bruise is gone and he's at full strength again. He had the whole weekend to heal, after all.

He'll probably kill me in gym. If you don't see an entry for Tuesday, March 23, it's probably because Vic stabbed me through the heart during fencing.

Dead man walking,

FINN REEDER

TUESDAY

March 23

I'm still alive.

Every student who isn't home sick has reported to the cafeteria. There are like ten of us. We'll be here all day, except for gym, according to Principal Toomey's announcement. All day is lunch, I guess.

It's just me and Vic, and Gas Mask is watching us.

Just watching. He (or she or whatever) never speaks anymore. He never even gets up from his chair. He just watches us.

I still don't know who Gas Mask is, but I know it's not Principal Toomey. The announcement came over the loudspeaker when Gas Mask was in the cafeteria with us, so it couldn't be him.

I bumped into Vic kind of on purpose. His arm still hurts. I took a big chance finding out, but I had to know. That's because I saw Coach Pangs before we got sent to the cafeteria.

He stopped me in the empty hall and put a hand on my shoulder. Then he leaned down and whispered right in my ear, "Dodge ball again, Reeder. Don't turn your back on Dooker." —

Then he walked off, laughing.

This flu has made everyone insane.

The only non-crazy one left,

FINN REEDER

WEDNESDAY

March 24

Vic is gone.

Gas Mask is gone.

Principal Toomey won't leave his office.

I spent the whole day in the gym with Coach Pangs.

"Sit!" he said when I walked in. So I sat down.

"Two words, Reeder," he barked at me. Even though he was across the gym, I could feel his spittle on my face.

Then he shouted: "Solo. Dodge ball."

I didn't have time to tell him that was three words. From behind his back, he pulled out a red rubber ball and launched it at my chest.

It slammed into me and I fell backward.

"Pick it up!" he shouted. I picked it up.

"Solo dodge ball!" Coach Pangs barked. "Begin!"

He blew his whistle.

I looked at him. He looked at me. I looked at the red ball. I turned to the bleachers, raised the ball, and heaved it with all my might.

The ball flew at the bleachers. It hit a bench about halfway up, bounced off, and went soaring toward the roof.

Coach Pangs and I watched it sail through the air. Then it started back down.

It came right at me. It fell at an amazing speed. I put out my hands, thinking I might catch it, but instead I just covered my face.

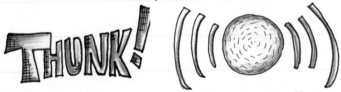

The ball struck my arms and bounced off. It rolled across the gym and stopped when it hit Coach Pangs in the foot.

"You're out!" he snapped. "Also, you won. Good game."

Dodge ball champion,

FINN REEDER

It hasn't been that bad, the last week or so. I mean, with the whole cafeteria staff out, we've been having whatever food Principal Toomey could get delivered. There was pizza that first day. We also had Mexican food, burgers and fries, and Chinese food.

You will inspire others with your good health.
Lucky Numbers: 1, 5, 8, 243

You will discover something amazing in 5 days.
Learn to speak Pig Latin! FISH ish-fay

Today, Coach Pangs and I left the gym after a few rounds of solo baseball, and something smelled . . . off.

Then we heard it. Metal was clanking on metal from behind the food line. Steam was wafting out of the kitchen too.

Then a head stuck out from the doorway. It was a very long, skinny head, with red hair covered by a hairnet.

"Doris!" Coach Pangs shouted.

"Hey, Coach!" Doris the lunch lady called back.

"Glad to see you're feeling better," the coach said.

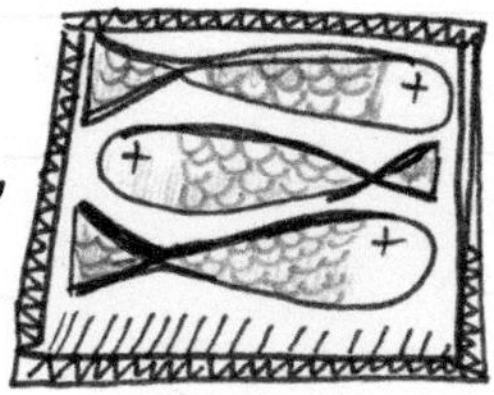

"You'll be even gladder when you get a taste of my Tuna Meatloaf Surprise!" Doris said.

Suddenly I wasn't feeling very good myself.

Skipping lunch,

FINN REEDER

You won't believe what happened today in gym, my only class. Henry Gluck and Gus Tattle walked in. They're not sick anymore.

Coach Pangs looked as surprised as I was. He didn't let it faze him, though. He just walked into the supply closet, grabbed two more red rubber balls, and gave us each one.

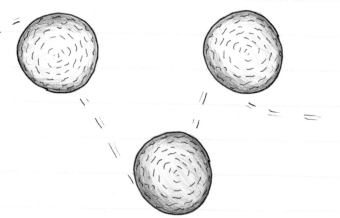

"Dodge ball," he said, smiling. "Every man for himself."

Then he blew his whistle.

kids in class: 3 (!!!)

Henry and Gus both looked at me. I realized a few things.

1. They had already had the flu.

2. I had not gotten the flu.

3. There were two of them and one of me.

So I put my ball on the ground. Henry and Gus threw at the same time. Henry's ball hit me in the belly, and Gus's ball hit me in the butt.

I didn't mind being the first one out. At least it was Friday.

Just before the final school bell, Principal Toomey came over the loudspeaker.

"The town council has just announced that a shipment of vaccines has arrived at the local clinic. All students and faculty who have not yet had this flu are expected to get vaccinated this weekend. That is all."

Coach Pangs blew his whistle. "Dismissed," he said. "And Finn Reeder, I will see you at the clinic tomorrow."

Not alone anymore,

FINN REEDER

So this morning, I was watching TV. Suddenly, a light went on in the hallway. I froze. A tall, slim figure appeared. She was wearing a long coat and holding a small black purse.

"Finn, put your shoes and jacket on. Time for you to get your vaccination."

It was my mom. She was healthy.

The shot wasn't actually that bad. I have a little bruise on my arm, but it's not as bad as Vic's was.

Coach Pangs was waiting for a shot when my mom and I were on our way out. "So, Finn," he said. "I guess just you and me managed to avoid the flu, huh?"

I nodded.

"Think fast!" he shouted. Then he pulled a red rubber ball from behind his back and threw it at my chest.

I don't know what came over me. Maybe I had super-strength from that vaccination.

Somehow, I caught that ball.

Coach Pangs opened his eyes wide in shock. He wasn't smiling.

I was, though. I lifted the ball, drew back, and launched it at him.

"Ahhh!" he cried. The ball struck him in the shoulder and bounced across the waiting room.

"Finn!" my mom said.

But Coach Pangs wasn't upset. He stepped forward and extended his hand.

I shook it.

"Good job, Finn," he said. "You have learned much about dodge ball."

I guess he was really proud of me. As my mom and I left, I heard him sniffle and blow his nose. I don't think it was because of the flu, either.

Teacher's pet,

FINN REEDER

This morning, maybe to make everyone feel better, Dad made pancakes.

Did I mention his fever is gone? It is. He was up at the crack of dawn, singing and everything. No more masks, no more hazmat suits. Life is back to normal at the Reeder house.

"I'm really impressed, Finn," Dad said over breakfast. "You must have been careful to avoid this flu. You probably washed your hands regularly. I know you wore that mask when you were around other people."

"Yes," I said. "I was pretty careful."

I don't know if I was any more careful than anyone else, really. I mean, Amy was careful, and she got sick.

Speaking of Amy, I also got an email from her today. She said her fever is gone and she'll be back in class on Monday. I wonder if we'll still draw cartoons together once all the other kids are back too.

Me and Amy

Relieved,

FINN REEDER

SO FAR:
Pizzas I ate: 7
Boxes of macaroni
and cheese I made: 4
Times Dad asked for
help wiping his nose: 3

Times
I helped: 1
(I learned my lesson)
Times I got the flu: 0

You have no idea how relieved I was to see a nearly full class today, with you in the front of the room, Ms. Westing.

And yes, part of the relief is because you said we don't have to keep doing this journal anymore. But it's also nice to have a teacher I can understand and who knows my name.

Just before class started, I took my normal seat in the back, next to Vic Dooker and behind Amy Fleur.

"Psst," Vic hissed at me. "Pssssst! Finn. Hey. Finn!"

"What?" I said out of the side of my mouth.

"I didn't get the flu," he said.

"Then why were you gone for two days last week?" I asked.

"My parents were both sick," he said, "so I had to stay home and make them soup."

kids in class: 12

RE BACK!

The bell rang to start class. "Why are you telling me this?" I whispered to Vic.

"I want you to know," he said, "you're not the only kid in town who didn't get sick."

I rolled my eyes. "Okay, Vic," I said.

If he wants to be proud of it, I'll let him. Amy didn't feel the same way.

"Hey, Vic," she said. Vic looked at her, and Amy lifted her fist.

"No!" Vic said. He put his head down on his desk and covered himself with his arms.

Amy just laughed.

By the way, I think I figured out who Gas Mask was! Vic says he knows who Gas Mask was. He thinks Gas Mask was an evil scientist who was responsible for H1N1. Amy says he's watched too many spy movies.

The detective,

FINN REEDER

TUESDAY
March 30

Okay, I know you said we don't have to keep this journal anymore. But I had one sheet of paper left, so I figured I might as well finish.

Also, I had a couple of things I wanted to include. You know, to wrap things up.

First of all, Principal Toomey called an assembly right away this morning, as you know. He said everything is back to normal. The cafeteria staff is back, all the teachers are back. Even Mr. Hearty, the gym teacher. Principal Toomey also said all our homework is due, and everyone groaned. I wonder if I'm the only student who actually kept a journal.

After the assembly, it was time for English. When I got there, you weren't in class yet. I went to the closet to get my notebook and put away my coat.

In the closet, behind all our coats, hanging on a hook, was a bright orange hazmat suit.

74

kids in class: 16

I had a feeling I was right.

I pulled a chair from a nearby desk. Vic kept watch at the door.

Amy stood beside the chair as I climbed on, so I could reach the top shelf. I still couldn't see up there, but I felt around and grabbed something.

"Here it is!" I said, and pulled it down.

The gas mask.

"No way!" Vic said.

"I told you it wasn't a mad scientist," Amy said.

"I didn't say 'mad,'" Vic said. "I said 'evil.'"

"Well, it doesn't matter which you said," I replied. "Because here's the proof. Gas Mask was Ms. Westing."

I'm right, aren't I, Ms. Westing? If you want me to keep it a secret, I will. In exchange for an A on my journal, that is.

Yours truly,

FINN REEDER

disinfectant (diss-in-FEK-tuhnt)—a chemical used to kill germs

epidemic (ep-uh-DEM-ik)—when a disease spreads quickly

hazmat (HAZ-mat)—a hazmat suit is made to withstand hazardous materials

infection (in-FEK-shuhn)—an illness caused by germs or viruses

influenza (in-floo-EN-zuh)—an illness that is caused by a virus. Flu symptoms are similar to those of a bad cold, plus fever and achiness.

outbreak (OWT-brake)—a sudden start of something

pandemic (pan-DEM-ik)—when a disease spreads to more than one continent or throughout the world

symptom (SIMP-tuhm)—something that shows that you have an illness

virus (VYE-ruhss)—a very tiny organism that can reproduce and grow only when inside living cells. Viruses cause diseases.

About the author: Eric Stevens lives in St. Paul, Minnesota. He enjoys video games and reading books. Some of his favorite things include pizza and trying new restaurants. Some of his least favorite things include olives and shoveling snow.

About the illustrator: Kay Fraser was born and raised in Buenos Aires, Argentina. Now she lives in Minnesota with her husband and two daughters. Kay loves dancing and reading and writing fantasy novels. She drinks at least four cups of coffee a day and really loves turkey sandwiches.

FINN'S GUIDE TO HAVING FUN EVEN IF YOU HAVE THE FLU OR EVERYONE ELSE DOES

1. Keep your own journal! For 30 days, record everything that happens. When you're done, you'll be amazed at all the crazy stuff that went on.
2. Create your own comic strip, like Amy and I did. Make up characters and have them go through crazy situations. (Be careful, though. If you want to stay out of trouble, you won't make your characters look like people you know.)
3. Write a story. Pretend that the main character, "Binn Heeder," is suffering through a worldwide pandemic. Does he get sick? Does he stay healthy? Who gets sick? Who doesn't? It's all up to you.

FIND YOUR GAS MASK AND PUT YOUR HAZMAT SUIT ON. THEN, IN A GROUP, DISCUSS:

1. How would you react if your school had a flu epidemic? What would you do differently?
2. In this book, some people started to behave strangely. Why do you think that happened?
3. What do you think happens on March 31?

Coach Pang's Guide to Solo Dodge Ball
1. Think defense. Your opponent wants to take you out. You need to stay in the game to survive.
2. Think offense. You need to take out your opponent before he or she takes you out first.
3. Watch your back. You never know what your opponent is thinking.
4. Strike first. Catch your opponent when he or she least expects it.
5. Expect the unexpected.

MEMO
To: Reeder family
From: Dad
This is a list of flu symptoms. Please circle the symptoms you currently are experiencing.
Then I can react appropriately. Thank you.

headache achiness fever red eyes fatigue
dry cough runny nose sore throat

VACCINE (vak-SEEN)—A substance containing dead, weakened, or living organisms that can be injected or taken orally or through the nose. A vaccine causes a person to produce antibodies that protect him or her from the disease caused by the organisms.

Basically, it tricks your body into thinking you have already had the disease.

ADVICE

MEMO
To: The School District
From: Principal Toomey

Students and teachers are advised to get the seasonal flu shot every year. Flu shots help protect you from seasonal influenza. They do not protect you from new strains like H1N1. (There are separate shots for those strains.) Each year, the flu shot is remade to attack flu strains scientists think may be spreading.

Young children, pregnant women, and the elderly are especially vulnerable to influenza and should get shots. So should medical professionals. Healthy adults may not need the flu shot, but it can help to stop the spread of disease.

If anyone has questions, they can find me in the principal's office.

Sincerely,

Principal G. Toomey

FINN'S TIPS FOR STAYING HEALTHY:

1. Wash your hands frequently, especially when you're out in public and before and after meals.
2. Wear a face mask to keep your germs from spreading to others.
3. Avoid public areas during flu season.
4. Stay calm. Panic causes stress, and when you're stressed, you're more likely to get sick. Really!!! (Look at my dad!)